The Child's World

Published in the United States of America by The Child's World®
1980 Lookout Drive • Mankato, MN 56003-1705
800-599-READ • www.childsworld.com

ACKNOWLEDGMENTS
The Child's World®: Mary Berendes, Publishing Director
The Design Lab: Kathleen Petelinsek, Design and Page Production
Literacy Consultants: Cecilia Minden, PhD, and Joanne Meier, PhD

LIBRARY OF CONGRESS
CATALOGING-IN-PUBLICATION DATA
Moncure, Jane Belk.
  My "u" sound box / by Jane Belk Moncure;
illustrated by Rebecca Thornburgh.
    p. cm. — (Sound box books)
  Summary: "Little u has an adventure with items beginning with
her letter's sound, such as umbrellas, an ugly duckling, and her
uncle the umpire."—Provided by publisher.
  ISBN 978-1-60253-161-1 (library bound : alk. paper)
  [1. Alphabet.] I. Thornburgh, Rebecca McKillip, ill. II. Title.
III. Series.
PZ7.M739Myu 2009   4195 1913 11/09
  [E]—dc22   2008033177

A NOTE TO PARENTS AND EDUCATORS:

Magic moon machines and five fat frogs are just a few of the fun things you can share with children by reading books with them. Reading aloud helps children in so many ways! It introduces them to new words, motivates them to develop their own reading skills, and expands their attention span and listening abilities. So it's important to find time each day to share a book or two . . . or three!

As you read with young children, you can help develop their understanding of how print works by talking about the parts of the book—the cover, the title, the illustrations, and the words that tell the story. As you read, use your finger to point to each word, modeling a gentle sweep from left to right.

Simple word games help develop important prereading skills, including an understanding of rhyme and alliteration (when words share the same beginning sound, such as "six" and "sand"). Try playing with words from a book you've just shared: "What other words start with the same sound as moon?" "Cat and hat, do those words rhyme?" The possibilities are endless—and so are the rewards!

My "u" Sound Box®

(This book concentrates on the short "u" sound in the story line. Words beginning with the long "u" sound are included at the end of the book.)

WRITTEN BY JANE BELK MONCURE

ILLUSTRATED BY REBECCA THORNBURGH

Little had a box. "I will find things that begin with my U sound," she said. "I will put them into my sound box."

"First, I will find an umbrella."

"I will run, run, run to find an umbrella."

Why did Little get under the box? Why was the box upside down?

Little found an umbrella. She

found lots of umbrellas.

She put one umbrella over her

head. Did she put the other

umbrellas into her box? She did.

Just then, the sun came out.

Little put the umbrella down.

But then the rain came down again.

Little put the umbrella up.

Then she saw some underclothes.

They were getting wet.

She took the underclothes off the

line. She put them into her box.

Little took the underclothes

upstairs. She put the

underclothes away.

"Now," she said, "I can play under my umbrella." She went

out in the rain.

"I can run through a puddle,"

she said. "What fun!"

Then she found an ugly duckling.

The ugly duckling was grumpy.

She put the ugly duckling into her box. "Do not be grumpy," she said.

"You will grow up to be beautiful."

Just then, her uncle came by.

He was getting wet, so Little gave her uncle an umbrella.

Then an umpire came by.

"Can you help us?" he said.

"We are playing baseball in the 🌂🌂 rain. We need umbrellas."

Little said, "I have a box full of umbrellas."

She gave the umpire an umbrella.

Then she gave everyone an umbrella.

What fun they had in the rain!

27

Little 's Word List

ugly duckling

uncle

umbrella

underclothes

umpire

upstairs

Other Words with the Short "u" Sound

udder

undershirt

urn

Uncle Sam

uphill

usher

Words with the Long "u" Sound

Little u has another sound in some words. She says her name, "u."
Can you read these words? Listen for Little u's name.

ukulele

unicycle

United States

unicorn

uniform

universe

More to Do!

Little ![girl] 's umbrellas kept everyone dry in the rain. You can make a toy umbrella with a little help from an adult.

What you need:

- a paper plate
- a drinking straw
- tape
- a pencil
- markers
- scissors

Directions:

1. Ask an adult to help you use the pencil to divide the paper plate into six triangle-shaped sections (like the slices of a pizza).

2. Use your markers to make each section a bright color.

3. Carefully cut a small hole in the center of the paper plate. Poke the plastic drinking straw in the hole and secure it with tape.

4. Now you have a fun toy umbrella with a little handle!
Hold your umbrella over your head and say this poem:

Rain

by Robert Louis Stevenson

The rain is falling all around
It falls on the field and tree,
It rains on the umbrellas here,
And on the ships at sea.

About the Author

Best-selling author Jane Belk Moncure has written over 300 books throughout her teaching and writing career. After earning a Master's degree in Early Childhood Education from Columbia University, she became one of the pioneers in that field. In 1956, she helped form the Virginia Association for Early Childhood Education, which established the first statewide standards for teachers of young children.

Inspired by her work in the classroom, Mrs. Moncure's books have become standards in primary education, and her name is recognized across the country. Her success is reflected not only in her books' popularity with parents, children, and educators, but also by numerous awards, including the 1984 C. S. Lewis Gold Medal Award.

About the Illustrator

Rebecca Thornburgh lives in a pleasantly spooky old house in Philadelphia. If she's not at her drawing table, she's reading—or singing with her band, called Reckless Amateurs. Rebecca has one husband, two daughters, and two silly dogs.